The Night Santa Got Lost

How NORAD Saved Christmas

By Michael Keane

Illustrated by Michael Garland

Cataloging-in-Publication data on file with the Library of Congress
ISBN 978-1-59698-810-1
Published in the United States by
Regnery Kids
An Imprint of Regnery Publishing, Inc.
One Massachusetts Avenue NW
Washington, DC 20001
www.Regnery.com

Manufactured in the United States of America
10 9 8 7 6 5 4 3 2 1
Books are available in quantity for promotional or premium use. Write to Director of Special Sales, Regnery Publishing, Inc., One Massachusetts Avenue NW, Washington, DC 20001, for information on discounts and terms, or call (202) 216-0600.

Distributed to the trade by
Perseus Distribution
250 West 57th Street
New York, NY 10107

DEDICATION

This book is dedicated to children around the world whose parents—Soldiers, Marines,
Airmen, Coast Guardsmen, and Sailors, as well as civilians and contractors—allow us
to live in a world where we have the freedom to believe in Santa Claus.
Including my friends' children...Ava, Blake, Ethan, Evelyn, Grace, Jase, Jason,
Jonathan, Katie, Koa, Megan, Samantha, Sasha, Sean, Stephen.

LUKE 2: 11–14
"For unto you is born this day in the city of David a Savior, who is Christ the Lord.
And this shall be a sign unto you; Ye shall find the babe wrapped in swaddling clothes, lying in a manger.
And suddenly there was with the angel a multitude of the heavenly host praising God, and saying,
Glory to God in the highest, and on earth peace, good will toward men."

'Twas the night before Christmas at NORAD's home base,
Not an airman was stirring, each one was in place,
Ready and waiting for the very first sight,
Of good old St. Nick on his Christmas Eve flight.

"To deter and detect, and defend the homeland—
North American Aerospace Defense Command!
It's our job to watch everything in the sky,
From airplanes to rockets—whatever can fly!"

On a day long ago began NORAD's tradition—
Tracking Santa's red sleigh on his once-a-year mission.
Using radar and satellites—fighter jets too!
Reporting on Santa, wherever he flew.

From Japan to Nepal, from New York to Phnom Penh,*
O'er the Great Wall of China and past London's Big Ben,
NORAD tracks Santa throughout his long flight,
While children sleep soundly, tucked in for the night.

*pronounced Nom Pen

But on this Christmas Eve, after quite a cold day,
There arose a huge blizzard, and it moved Santa's way.
"This might be a problem," said a sergeant with fear.
"That wind seems too strong for eight tiny reindeer."

Much farther away, in the Arctic North Pole,
The elves worked quite hard, they had only one goal:
To hitch up the reindeer and pack up the sleigh,
With presents for children so far, far away.

Santa finished his list of those naughty and nice,
He pulled on his red suit and then checked the list twice.
"We'd better get going, this storm's getting stronger.
We must leave right now, we can't wait here much longer."

Back at NORAD's HQ the news came like a shock—
"Santa just left, way ahead of the clock!
Commence tracking Santa, his flight's so erratic.
He's fighting fierce headwinds right off the Atlantic!"

And then as they watched, the green blip disappeared.
No sign of Santa, nor a single reindeer!
"The radar's lost Santa!" they cried in a panic.
"We must find him now, or this will be gigantic!"

The General, a four star, ran straight to the base.
He was huffing and puffing and had a red face.
"Where was Santa last spotted?" he said, and he frowned.
He pulled out some maps, and all gathered around.

The Commander-in-Chief was handed a phone,
"Scramble the fighter jets! Send up a drone!
For both red state and blue state, this is a real threat!
It's even much worse than our national debt!"

Jet fighters took off from their base with a scream.
They flew to the place where the blip was last seen.
They used their night vision, then they tried infrared.
"Hey, look at that there, does that look like a sled?"

A squad fast-roped down to the white ice below.
They searched for eight reindeer while crunching through snow.
"Hey Dasher? Hey Dancer? Hey Prancer and Vixen?
Where's Comet? Where's Cupid? Where's Donner and Blitzen?"

Ahead they saw something, a blinking red light,
They dug through the snow, and they found quite a sight—
A cold, shaken Santa and eight shivering deer.
"NORAD's found Santa!" they reported with cheer.

But Santa was worried for the world's girls and boys.
"There's not enough time left to get them their toys!
I'm so far behind now, how can it be done?
No toys Christmas morning? That's not very fun!"

Then the generals met, and they hatched quite a plan.
They would call every base, from right here to Japan—
"Canada and NATO, our allies help too.
We'll all work together, one big happy crew.

"We've got battleships, cruisers, and fast submarines,
'Copters, and cargo jets, like C-17s.
Big trucks and Strykers and personnel carriers,
Huge armored tanks that can climb over barriers."

Then NORAD showed Santa its satellite photos,
Of rooftops and chimneys where Santa Claus goes.
"Our agency knows on a need-to-know basis,
Who's been naughty and nice…Whoa! They're classified cases."

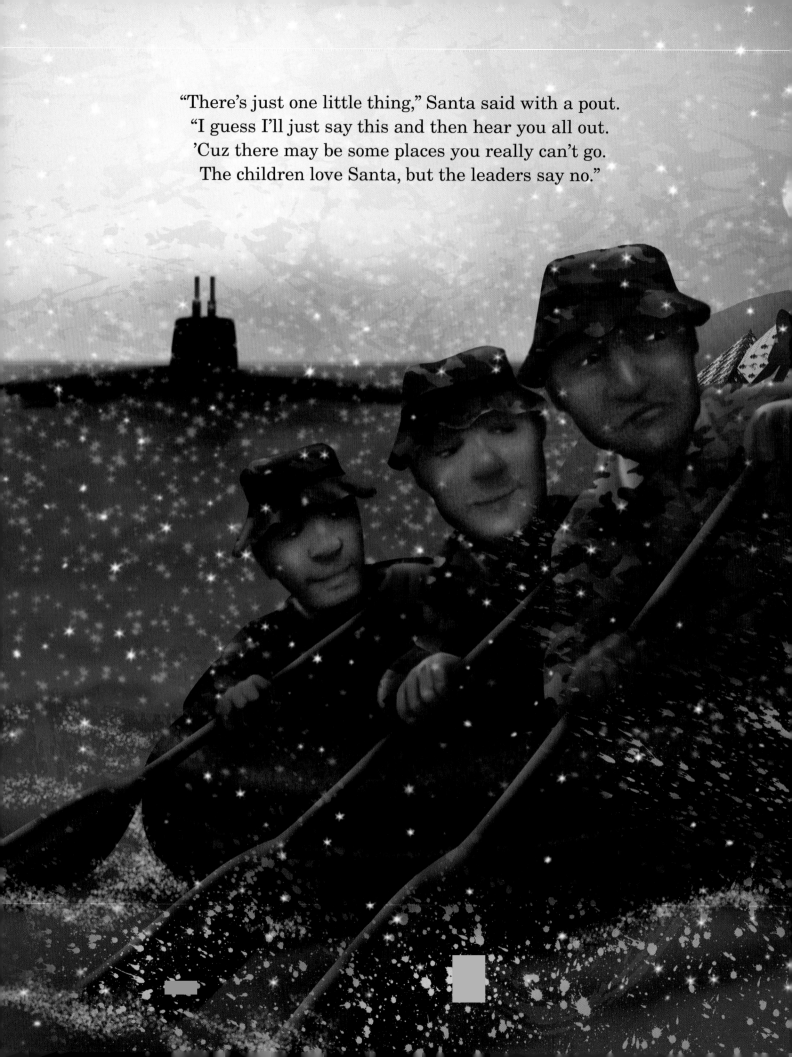

"There's just one little thing," Santa said with a pout.
"I guess I'll just say this and then hear you all out.
'Cuz there may be some places you really can't go.
The children love Santa, but the leaders say no."

Santa then learned a secret that very few know…
"We have Special Ops teams that can come in quite low—
Delta Force, Navy SEALs, and tough Army Rangers.
In those types of places, they'll handle the dangers!"

Santa paused and he nodded. All knew what that meant.
"In the spirit of Christmas, I give my consent.
I've delivered these toys for a hundred odd years.
With this very bad storm I will need volunteers."

"Go Army! Go Marines! Go Navy and Air Force!
Call in the Reservists and the Guardsmen, of course!
To the ends of the earth, help with Santa's big haul!
Now march away! Fly away! Sail away, all!"

Then soldiers and airmen all went right to work,
Captains by privates, first sergeants by clerks.
Shoulder to shoulder, they worked through the night.
They brought toys by Humvees, dropped others by flight.

When the last package went to the very last child,
Santa turned to the troops with a look that beguiled.
He started to smile, tears dampened his cheek,
And the soldiers saluted, but no one dared speak.

Santa leapt to his sleigh, quite pleased with the night.
"'Tis the best Christmas yet!" he exclaimed with delight.
"You have come to the rescue, and saved this great day.
Merry Christmas to all!" Then he lifted away!

Wrapping It Up

· · · · · A Christmas Tradition Begins · · · · ·

"Hey, kiddies! Call me on my private phone and I will talk to you personally any time day or night." So read an ad placed by a local Sears department store in 1955. It was intended as an invitation from none other than Santa Claus himself. But the phone number listed in the ad was off by a digit. Instead of reaching Santa at the North Pole, children were dialing in to a top secret phone line designated to ring only if the Soviet Union was attacking the U.S.

Imagine the surprise when U.S. Air Force Colonel Harry Shoup, fearing the worst, picked up the phone and heard a tiny voice ask, "Is this Santa Claus?"

Before long, the phone was ringing off the hook. Shoup, then director of operations at CONAD (the Continental Air Defense Command—NORAD's predecessor), decided to offer the young callers information about Santa's progress from the North Pole, and thus the NORAD Santa tracking tradition was born.

Every year since, NORAD has offered annual Santa tracking as a service to the world's children. Everyone is invited to call in, especially on December 24, to check on Santa's whereabouts.

You can join in the fun online at **http://www.noradsanta.org**.

Wrapping It Up

· · · · · NORAD · · · · ·

In case you are wondering, NORAD is a very real and very important defense operation. NORAD (North American Aerospace Defense Command) is a joint United States and Canadian military organization. NORAD monitors the air and space over North America to detect and warn of any danger to North America from aircraft, missiles, or satellites. NORAD's job is non-stop and involves using a worldwide system of sensors—radar, satellites, and aircraft—to accomplish its very important mission. NORAD's headquarters are located at Peterson Air Force Base in Colorado.

For more information, visit **http://www.norad.mil**.

Other important military organizations mentioned in the story include:

· · · · · US Transportation Command · · · · ·

If Santa Claus needed help delivering his toys, he would most likely turn to the United States Transportation Command—TRANSCOM. Its mission is to provide air, land, and sea transportation for America's military both in times of peace and war. TRANSCOM is responsible for deploying military members around the world and providing them with whatever they need to sustain them during their mission. TRANSCOM moves people, their property, petroleum, weapons, ammunition, and other cargo. TRANSCOM uses military and commercial trucks, trains, railcars, aircraft, ships, and information systems to accomplish its missions. During an average week, TRANSCOM conducts more than 1,900 air missions, with 25 ships underway and 10,000 ground shipments. TRANSCOM operates in 75 percent of the world's countries.

For more information, visit **http://www.transcom.mil**.

Wrapping It Up

• • • • • US Special • • • • •
Operations Command

Special Operations Command is responsible for the United States'
"special mission units" including Delta Force, Navy SEALs, Army Rangers,
Marine Special Operations Forces, the Night Stalkers (a special aviation
regiment), and the Air Force's 24th Special Tactics Squadron. These
are highly trained warriors who perform special missions such as
counterterrorism and training the military forces of friendly nations.
    For more information, visit **http://www.socom.mil**.

• • • • • • The United States • • • • • •
Defense Department

The Army, Navy, and Marine Corps were established during the American
Revolution. The War Department was established in 1789, while the Coast
Guard, part of Homeland Security in peace time, was established in 1790.
This was followed by the founding of the Department of the Navy in 1798.
The decision to unify the different services under one
department led to the creation of the National Military Establishment in 1947. This establishment
would replace the War Department. The three
military branches, Army, Navy, and Air Force,
were placed under the direct control of the
new Secretary of Defense, confirmed by the
Senate.
    In 1949, the National Military Establish-
ment was renamed the Department of Defense.
For more information, visit
http://www.defense.gov.

Wrapping It Up

• • • • • Christmas in • • • • •
Military History

On Christmas night in 1776, George Washington led his rag tag troops across the icy Delaware River to engage an enemy army that was sated and fast asleep after enjoying a Christmas dinner. After some initial fighting, most of the enemy surrendered. Perhaps they were too full to fight? This dramatic victory inspired Washington's army and attracted new recruits to fight for the American Revolution.

• • • • •

On Christmas Eve in 1863, Tad Lincoln pleaded with his father to spare the life of a turkey that was intended to be eaten for Christmas dinner. Tad had named the turkey Jack and considered him to be a pet. President Lincoln wrote out a formal pardon and spared the life of the turkey. It has since become a presidential tradition, and now it is done every Thanksgiving.

• • • • •

In 1914, before the entry of the United States into World War I, there was an unofficial but notable Christmas truce that spontaneously occurred between the soldiers fighting at the front lines. On Christmas Eve German troops began decorating their areas by placing candles on trenches and Christmas trees. When they began singing Christmas carols, the British responded by singing carols of their own. Soon the two sides ventured forth, exchanging small presents such as food and drink. The peaceful exchanges lasted throughout Christmas day and even longer in some areas of the battlefield.

• • • • •

Wrapping It Up

After the end of World War II, tensions grew between the Soviet Union and the United States. East Germany was controlled by the Soviets after the end of the war. West Berlin was controlled by the United States, Great Britain, and France. East Berlin was controlled by the Soviets. But Berlin was located in Soviet-controlled East Germany. In June 1948, the Soviet leader, Joseph Stalin, decided to cut off all rail and auto traffic to West Berlin for America and its allies.

The people in West Berlin would starve if supplies could not be brought into the city. Led by the United States, a massive air supply operation was launched to fly food into the city of 2.5 million people. Tons of food and fuel were supplied every day by brave pilots who flew under difficult conditions, including bad weather and harassment by Soviet aircraft. One American pilot became very popular with the children of Berlin: Lieutenant Colonel Gail S. Halvorsen of the United States Air Force. Halvorsen made small parachutes from handkerchiefs. Each parachute carried a bundle of candy that he would drop from his plane. The children could recognize his plane because he would wiggle the plane's wings at them. He became know to the children of Berlin as "Uncle Wiggly Wings" and "the Candy Bomber."

As Christmas approached, American soldiers wrote home asking people to send toys to be delivered to the 10,000 children of Berlin. It became known as "Operation Santa Claus." Soon American children all over the country were buying presents and sending them to Germany. Many of the presents were wrapped with messages like this: "To a little German boy my age" and signed "Johnny age 12." On Christmas day, every child in Berlin received a toy from Operation Santa Claus.

• • • • •

Wrapping It Up

In October 1961, during the height of the Cold War between the United States and the Soviet Union, the Soviets tested a nuclear bomb in the Arctic Circle, not far from the North Pole. News of the bomb testing greatly distressed an eight-year-old girl, Michelle Rochon, from Michigan. She wrote a letter to President John F. Kennedy asking him, "Please stop the Russians from bombing the North Pole because they will kill Santa Claus."

President Kennedy wrote back to the third grader telling her, "You must not worry about Santa Claus, I talked with him yesterday and he is fine. He will be making the rounds this year."

• • • • •

Several days before Christmas in 1967, President Lyndon Johnson made a surprise visit to Southeast Asia. He expressed gratitude to the troops for their courage and sacrifice and presented medals to many wounded soldiers. From Vietnam President Johnson then headed to the Vatican where he met with Pope Paul VI, asking for his help for better treatment of American prisoners of war. The two men discussed proposals for resolving the war in Vietnam. Speaking of his Christmas trip Johnson said, "No man can avoid being moved to try harder for peace at Christmastime."

• • • • •

On Christmas day in 2008, in his last official trip as Commander-in-Chief before he left office, President Bush made a surprise visit to American troops in Iraq. Air Force One, the president's special aircraft, was renamed "Rudolph One" for the trip.

He concluded a speech to the troops by saying, "They ask me what I'm going to miss as the President. I'll tell you what I'm going to miss: being the Commander-in-Chief of such a fabulous group of folks. May God bless you, and God bless America."

About the Author and Illustrator

Michael Keane is a Fellow of National Security at the Pacific Council on International Policy. He was embedded in Iraq with the U.S. Army's 101st Airborne Division, under the command of General David Petraeus, and in Kabul, Afghanistan, at the headquarters of the ISAF Commander, General Stanley McChrystal. Keane is a former Fellow of the U.S. Department of Defense's National Security Education Program. He has appeared on CNN, CNBC, Fox News, and The History Channel, and has been profiled in *BusinessWeek* magazine. Keane is also the author of *PATTON: Blood, Guts, and Prayer* and the *Dictionary of Modern Strategy and Tactics*. He earned his JD from the University of Texas School of Law, an MBA from the University of Chicago, and a BA from the University of Southern California. He lives in Santa Monica, California.

Michael Garland, an award-winning author and illustrator, has been on the *New York Times* Best Seller list four times! His work includes *Miss Smith's Incredible Storybook*, which recently won the California and Delaware State Reading awards, and *Christmas Magic*, now a season classic and currently being developed for a TV special. Garland has illustrated for celebrity authors like James Patterson and Gloria Estefan. His illustrations for Patterson's *SantaKid* were the inspiration for Saks Fifth Avenue's Christmas holiday window display in New York City. His work has won many honors and is frequently included in the Society of Illustrators and the Original Art of Children's book show, as well as annuals from *Print*, *Graphis*, and *Communications Arts* magazines. You can learn more about Michael Garland at his website http://www.garlandpicturebooks.com.

Acknowledgments

I would like to express my greatest appreciation to the entire team at Regnery Kids, especially to Marji Ross who worked so quickly to bring this book to life, Diane Reeves who may still be counting syllables to make sure the rhyme pattern is perfect, Cheryl Barnes for artfully bringing the story to life, and Rebekah Meinecke for her marketing expertise.

Semper Fi to my brother and hero, Lieutenant Colonel John Keane, USMC, who gladly read the book's first draft on Christmas Day… perhaps he had some good feedback from Katie who is (almost) always on Santa's nice list.

I greatly appreciate the feedback and encouragement of the Clearwater family, especially the intelligent and charming Angela and Rose, each of whom listened attentively while I nervously read them the book as it neared completion.

I am also eternally grateful to Stephen Breimer of Bloom Hergott for his friendship, intelligence, and unflappable nature, Samantha Tang for her advice and assistance, and to Lawrence Schiller and The Norman Mailers Writers Colony for their encouragement of aspiring writers.

A special thanks to all my friends who have served the U.S. military in the important field of public affairs and communications. You have all helped me in too many ways to count—Kevin Aandahl, Tracy Bailey, Duncan Boothby, Greg Bishop, Kimberly Brubeck, Cynthia Bauer, John Clearwater, Joyce Creech, Carol Darby, Jennifer Elzea, Erik Gunhus, Greg Julian, Staci Reidinger, Kanessa Trent, Tadd Sholtis, and Stewart Upton.

And of course, thank you, Michael Garland, for your vivid and playful illustrations!